Two in One

A WISH TOO FAR

and

PUFFCHEEK'S PALACE

ILLUSTRATED BY LESLEY SMITH

P
· PARRAGON ·

This is a Parragon Book

©Parragon 1997

Parragon
13-17 Avonbridge Trading Estate
Atlantic Road, Avonmouth
Bristol. BS11 9QD

Produced by The Templar Company plc,
Pippbrook Mill, London Road, Dorking,
Surrey RH4 1JE

Designed by Janie Louise Hunt
Edited by Caroline Steeden
Printed and bound in Italy
ISBN 0 75252 499 2

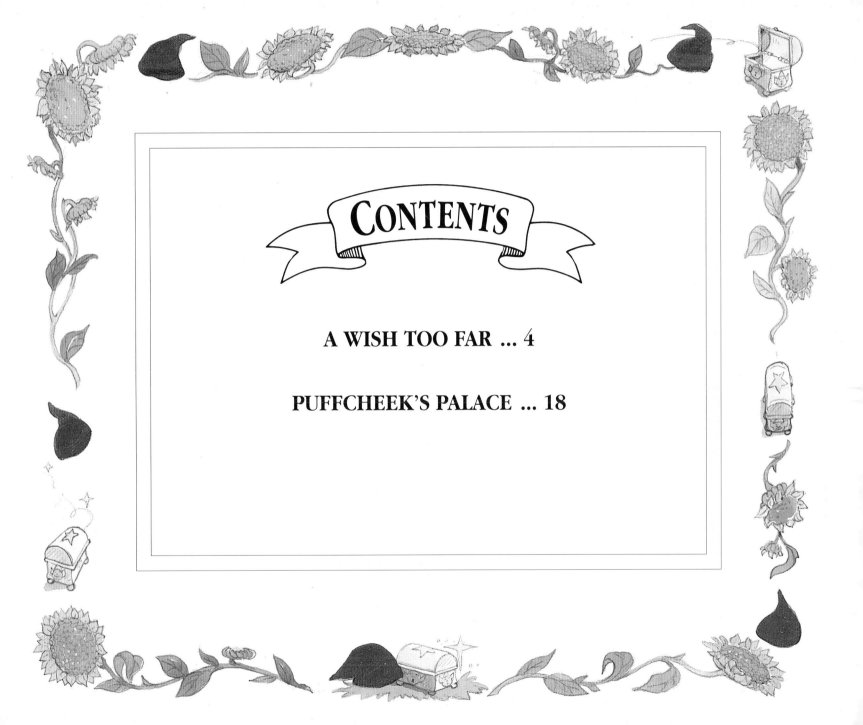

CONTENTS

A WISH TOO FAR ... 4

PUFFCHEEK'S PALACE ... 18

A WISH TOO FAR

WRITTEN BY DAVE KING

Nathan was bored. He wasn't just bored in that "Ho Hum! I haven't got a thing to do!" kind of way that most of us feel every now and then. Oh no, he was bored in a full blown, major league, top of the list, wet Sunday afternoon in a boring seaside town kind of way, that makes you pace around for an hour and a half before screaming, "IIIIII'm boooorrred!!" at the top of your voice.

Strangely enough, it was a wet Sunday afternoon in a boring seaside town. Nathan's parents had brought him

here with talk of a "lovely week in a delightful town by the sea." So far, the "lovely" and "delightful" parts of his parents' description had most definitely failed to appear. Certainly, they had spent the better part of a week in a town by the sea (which was a distinctly murky shade of grey, by the way), but "lovely" and "delightful"? No, these weren't the words that sprang into Nathan's mind. It had, after all, rained for half the time and poured with rain for the other half. The gloomy atmosphere that hung over the town was like the feeling you get when you're waiting for a kiss from a particularly ugly, long lost aunt!

Making matters worse was the fact that his little sister, Janine, and his little brother, Christian, were having a lovely time playing happily together. The miserable weather didn't seem to bother them. They were just as happy to play indoors.

Nathan just wanted the holiday to be over and to get back home. Unfortunately, they still had another two days to go. Nathan paced up and down, sat grumpily in a chair (ignoring the book that his dad had bought for him), or sat in front of the television, flicking between the channels. And still the rain pitter-pattered against the window.

"I wish I could be on my own somewhere, without my family getting under my feet!" he thought, gloomily.

Finally, he got up and grabbed his coat. "Where are you going?" asked his mum.

"Into the garden!" he replied.

His mum sighed wearily. "But it's still raining!"

Nathan put on his coat.

"I don't care!" he said. "I'm going to stand in the garden and grow roots and become a tree and then I'll be stuck here for ever!" And with that, he stomped out.

"Cor!" said Janine, excitedly. "That sounds brilliant! Come on, Chris, let's go and watch!"

Out in the garden, Nathan splashed across the muddy grass with his sister and brother following closely behind. As they neared the far end of the garden, Nathan turned to the others and began to snarl at them, continuing to walk backwards as he did so.

"Why don't you leave me alone?" he snapped.

"We want to see you turn into a tree!" Christian replied.

"Ohhh… that's all I need…" Nathan began, but was cut off as he disappeared from sight. Janine and Christian stopped in their tracks.

They looked down and saw a hole in the ground where Nathan had been walking. Peering down into it, they jumped back with shock as Nathan's head popped up.

"Aaaaahhhh!" they screamed in unison.

"It's okay!" replied Nathan. "The hole wasn't very deep! And look what I found down there…"

Nathan held up a small, shiny box that gleamed and sparkled, even in the gloomy rain.

"What is it?" Janine asked.

Just as she spoke, the box slipped from Nathan's fingers and landed on the wet grass. The lid flipped open and a twinkly swirl of light flew into the air. The children gasped in amazement, as a tiny figure materialised in front of them. A man, no more than five or six inches tall, hovered in the air before landing on a nearby sunflower. He had a bushy white beard and was wearing a pointed red hat.

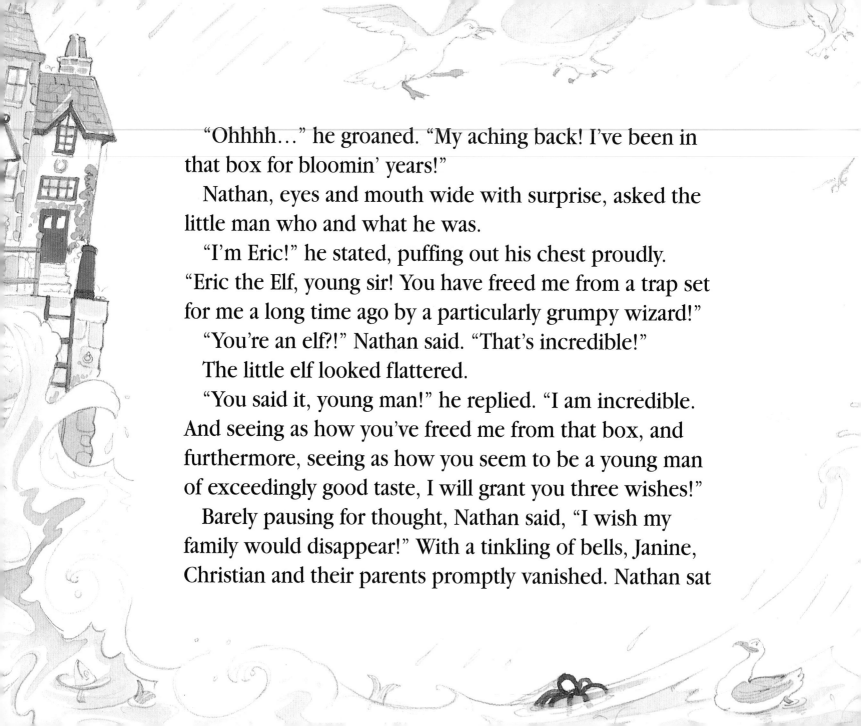

"Ohhhh…" he groaned. "My aching back! I've been in that box for bloomin' years!"

Nathan, eyes and mouth wide with surprise, asked the little man who and what he was.

"I'm Eric!" he stated, puffing out his chest proudly. "Eric the Elf, young sir! You have freed me from a trap set for me a long time ago by a particularly grumpy wizard!"

"You're an elf?!" Nathan said. "That's incredible!"

The little elf looked flattered.

"You said it, young man!" he replied. "I am incredible. And seeing as how you've freed me from that box, and furthermore, seeing as how you seem to be a young man of exceedingly good taste, I will grant you three wishes!"

Barely pausing for thought, Nathan said, "I wish my family would disappear!" With a tinkling of bells, Janine, Christian and their parents promptly vanished. Nathan sat on the wet grass, not quite believing what had happened.

"Is… is that it?" he asked. "Are they r…really gone?"

Eric gestured around the garden. "Look around you !" he said. Certainly, Janine and Christian were no longer there. Eric leant forwards and prodded Nathan. "Listen, sonny, I'm a busy elf! What's your second wish?"

"I wish I was somewhere nice and hot, all by myself!" Nathan answered. And suddenly, he was alone on a beautiful beach, the blue sky arching high over his head and the sea glittering like polished diamonds and stretching away for ever.

"Wow!" Nathan said, getting to his feet and running across the hot sand. "This is brilliant, eh, Eric? Eric?" There was no answer. Nathan whirled around quickly, looking everywhere. "Eric?" he shouted again, but there was no reply, only the sound of the sea, lapping gently at the shore.

He ran around for what seemed like ages, but the empty beach seemed to have no end, and the tropical forest that bordered the beach looked a bit dark and scary.

Finally, hot, tired and more than a little worried, he flopped down on the sand and began to sob quietly. If only he could be back with all his family around him in that funny little bungalow on the edge of the wet and dreary seaside town!

"Well, I'm sure that can be arranged!" said a little voice at Nathan's side, making him jump. It was Eric. "You said you wanted to be alone, so I thought I'd give you a little time to yourself!"

"I want to go back and I want my family to be back with me!" Nathan said, breathlessly.

"And is that your third and final wish, then?" Eric asked. Nathan nodded his head vigorously.

"Oh, it is! It is!" he said.

"I'll see what I can do," said Eric.

Janine tugged at his arm and Nathan felt the rain against his face. "Come up out of that hole!" she said, as she and Christian peered down at him. Nathan climbed out of the damp hole and looked around, feeling very glad to be back. He could see his mum and dad inside the house and thought to himself that it was one of the nicest sights he had ever seen.

"Your brother and sister won't remember me!" Eric said, appearing in front of Nathan. "But I think you will, and you'll remember what you learnt today!"

"You bet!" Nathan said. "I'll never take my family for granted again! Even if they do bring me for a lovely week in a delightful town by the sea!"

And as Eric twinkled from sight, Nathan looked up at the grey sky, took his sister's hand, and ran inside laughing to join his family!

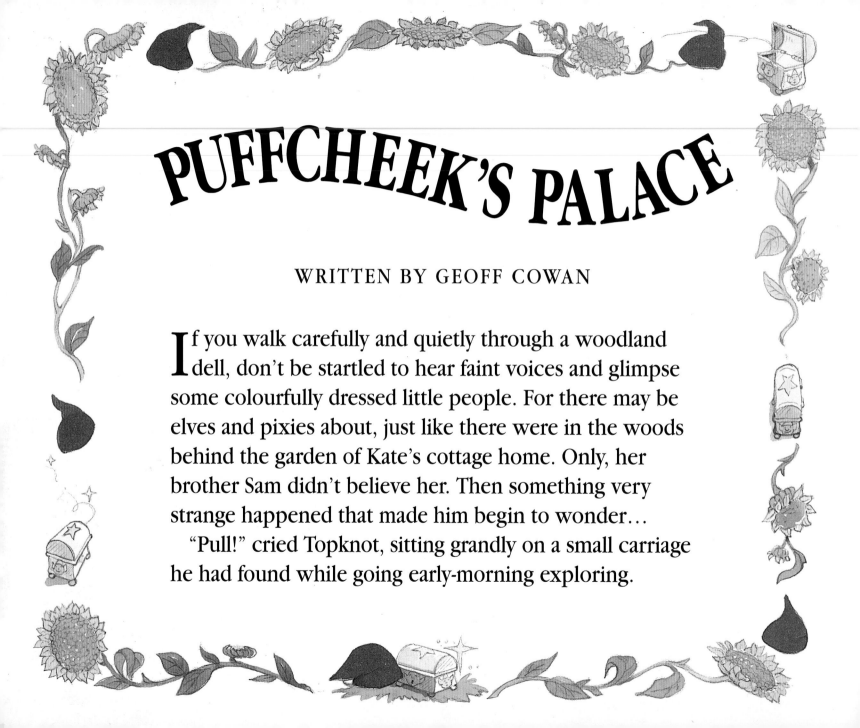

PUFFCHEEK'S PALACE

WRITTEN BY GEOFF COWAN

If you walk carefully and quietly through a woodland dell, don't be startled to hear faint voices and glimpse some colourfully dressed little people. For there may be elves and pixies about, just like there were in the woods behind the garden of Kate's cottage home. Only, her brother Sam didn't believe her. Then something very strange happened that made him begin to wonder…

"Pull!" cried Topknot, sitting grandly on a small carriage he had found while going early-morning exploring.

He had fetched the other elves, and they were using a rope of woven grass to tow his discovery away. However, nothing much happened in those woods without the sharp-eyed pixies noticing. When they saw the carriage, they wanted to join in the fun.

"Push!" shouted Puffcheek to his fellow pixies.

So the elves pulled the carriage while the pixies pushed, until it lurched and Topknot almost fell off.

"Pulling's safer than pushing me along!" he called, grumpily.

"But pushing's easier, especially if you go downhill!" protested Puffcheek. "Watch! We'll show you!"

Before Topknot could stop them, Puffcheek and the other pixies gave such a mighty shove that the carriage suddenly sped forward. It moved so fast that the startled elves hardly had time to jump out of the way.

Now, Topknot did topple off. He landed safely and softly on the thick grass while the carriage hurtled into a deep ditch and overturned, its wheels spinning in the air.

"That was your fault, Puffcheek!" snapped Topknot. "When it comes to being useful, pixies should learn a lesson from elves!"

Suddenly, heavy footsteps saved an argument as they all raced for cover.

"There it is!" cried Kate, pointing. "What a place to leave your skateboard!"

"I didn't!" replied Sam. "I told you! I put it down by a tree at the edge of the woods while I collected some conkers that had fallen. I couldn't carry everything home in one go. Then Mum called us for tea and I forgot all about my skateboard until today. Someone must have moved it!"

"Pixies and elves, I suppose!" smiled Kate.

Sam laughed and scrambled into the ditch. He picked up his skateboard, then headed for home. Kate was about to follow when she spotted the elves' grass rope that had broken free from the skateboard. Kate looked at it thoughtfully and put it in her pocket.

"So that's where the carriage came from," said Topknot, afterwards.

"You mean skateboard," corrected Puffcheek. "The Big People use all kinds of odd things and give them some very funny names!"

"Well, whatever they call it, I want it back!" cried Topknot. "Finders keepers. That's only fair!"

Even the pixies agreed, so Puffcheek had no choice but to try and recover the skateboard.

Which brought him to Kate's cottage garden. Sam had already gone to meet a friend, taking the skateboard with him. Meanwhile, Kate sat at the far end of the garden to examine the little grass rope. Puffcheek crept closer, searching for the skateboard. Suddenly, Kate sneezed and blew the pixie off a log he had clambered on to.

"Hey! Look out, clumsy!" he yelled and Kate was just close enough to hear.

"Oh, there really are pixies," she cried. "Did you make this rope!"

"No, it was the elves!" replied Puffcheek, picking himself up.

Then he remembered how much larger Big People were and was about to hurry away. It was only the thought of facing an angry Topknot without the skateboard that stopped him.

"I'll weave you a grass bracelet if you give me that carriage, er, skateboard," said Puffcheek.

"I was right! You did move it!" said Kate. "But the skateboard's not mine!"

Puffcheek explained what had happened. Then he sighed, "I can't return empty-handed to Topknot!"

Kate remembered something and had an idea. "Come back as the sun goes down and I may be able to help!"

Unbeknown to Kate, Sam had arrived home and come into the garden.

"Who were you talking to?" he asked Kate, puzzled.

"Oh, just a pixie!" she replied, playfully.

"You know you tidied up your cupboard yesterday. Didn't you say you wanted to get rid of your toy castle?" Kate asked.
Sam nodded. "I'm too big for it now!"

"I know someone who's just the right size!" said Kate.
"Can I have it?"
"If you like," said Sam.

When Sam went inside, Kate fetched the little castle, complete with its turrets, drawbridge and battlements. She took it to the edge of the wood. At dusk, Puffcheek found the castle with a note from Kate telling him it was for Topknot.

"I'm sorry I was cross with you, Puffcheek!" said Topknot as, this time, the elves and pixies happily pushed and pulled the toy castle deeper into the woods. "A castle's better than a carriage any day!"

"You can call it 'Topknot's Castle'," said Puffcheek. "Or 'Puffcheek's Palace'," replied Topknot kindly. "It's yours as long as we can play inside and have parties there! After all, you were very brave to speak to one of the Big People!"

Puffcheek smiled proudly as the elves and pixies congratulated him.

Next morning, before school, Sam followed his sister into the garden.

"I saw you carrying my castle down to the bottom of the garden last night," he said. "You wanted to play with it yourself all along, didn't you?"

"No, I left it here," replied Kate, pointing. "But it's gone!"

"Just like my skateboard," said Sam, thoughtfully. "Shall we search for it?"

"No," replied Kate, who was very pleased to have helped Puffcheek and the others.

"Don't tell me you think the elves and pixies took my old toy castle too!" grinned Sam.

Kate nodded. "Who else?" she smiled. "Only, this time, I think we'll let them keep it!"